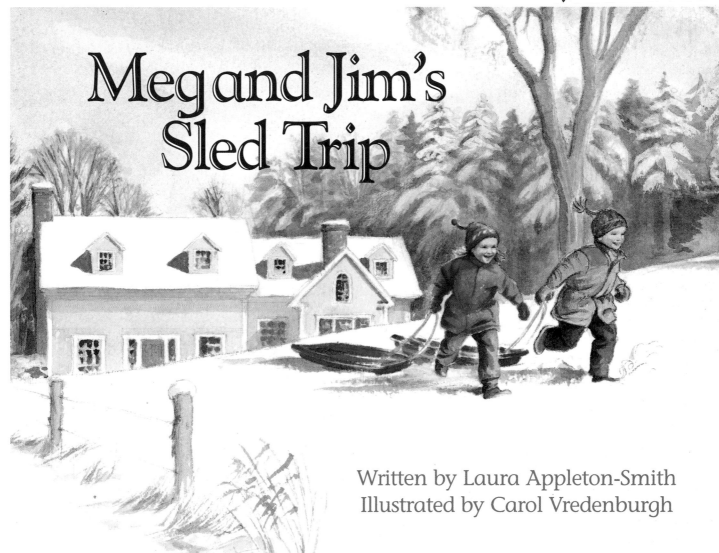

Meg and Jim's Sled Trip

Written by Laura Appleton-Smith

Illustrated by Carol Vredenburgh

Laura Appleton-Smith grew up sledding on the hills of Vermont.
She holds a degree in English from Middlebury College. Laura is a primary schoolteacher who has combined her talents in creative writing with her experience in early childhood education to create *Books to Remember*.
She lives in New Hampshire where she still enjoys sledding on a beautiful winter's day.

Carol Vredenburgh graduated Summa Cum Laude from Syracuse University and has worked as an artist and illustrator ever since. Now happily settled in New Hampshire, Carol hopes that her love of New England will come across in each picture, and will inspire and uplift each reader.

A Book to Remember™

Published by Flyleaf Publishing
Post Office Box 287, Lyme, NH 03768

For orders or information, contact us at **(800) 449-7006**.
Please visit our website at **www.flyleafpublishing.com**

Second printing, revised
Library of Congress Catalog Card Number: 98-96631
Hardcover ISBN-13: 978-0-9658246-0-6
Hardcover ISBN-10: 0-9658246-0-8
Softcover ISBN-13: 978-0-9658246-5-1
Softcover ISBN-10: 0-9658246-5-9

This book is dedicated to the town of Lyme, New Hampshire.

LAS & CV

Meg and Jim and Mom and Dad sit snug in the den as the wind gusts and the snow drifts outside.

At last, the wind and snow stop.

The sun is out and a blanket of snow is
on top of the land.

Meg and Jim get dressed to sled.

They put on snow pants and jackets.

They put on mittens and hats, too.

They drag their red sleds past the elm tree
to the top of the big sled hill.

"Get set, go!" yells Jim as he jumps in his sled.

Meg jumps in her sled too.

The sleds go fast down the hill.

When they stop, Meg and Jim jump up and run back to the top.

Their red sleds zigzag on the snow as they drag them up the hill.

On the next trip Jim jumps in the back of Meg's sled.

The sled goes faster and faster until it spins and hits a big snow drift.

The sled jumps up and lands with a bump...

… and dumps Meg and Jim in the soft snow.

Meg and Jim have snow on their hats and on their jackets.

They have snow down their necks and in their mittens!

Up and down and up and down
they go until they have to rest.

Meg and Jim sit on top of the hill.

The sun glints on the trees that
are dusted with windswept snow.

Meg and Jim drag their sleds back past the elm tree.

When they get in they undress and hang their jackets and snow pants on pegs.

They put their wet hats and mittens on the rack.

Meg and Jim and Mom and Dad snack on muffins and sip mugs of hot drinks.

Meg and Jim tell Mom and Dad about their sled runs and jumps and bumps.

Meg and Jim had fun in the snow.

Meg and Jim's Sled Trip is decodable with the knowledge of the 26 phonetic alphabet sounds and the ability to blend those sounds together.

Puzzle Words are words used in the story that are either irregular or have sound/spelling correspondences that the reader may not be familiar with.

The **Puzzle Word Review List** contains Puzzle Words that have been introduced in previous books in the *Books to Remember* Series.

Please Note: If all of the words on this page are pre-taught and the reader knows the 26 phonetic alphabet sounds, and has the ability to blend those sounds together, this book is 100% phonetically decodable.

Puzzle Words

outside
about
too
their
them
go
goes
are
have
snow
put
tree

Puzzle Word Review List

the
out
they
her
he
to
that
down
when
with
a
of

"er"/"ed" Endings

dress**ed**
fast**er**
dust**ed**

Decodable Vocabulary

Meg	hats	soft
Jim	drag	necks
and	red	rest
Mom	past	glints
Dad	elm	windswept
sit	top	undress
snug	big	hang
in	hill	pegs
den	drift	wet
as	sleds	rack
wind	set	snack
gusts	yells	muffins
drifts	jumps	sip
at	his	mugs
last	fast	hot
stop	up	drinks
sun	run	tell
is	back	had
blanket	zigzag	fun
on	next	Meg's
top	trip	
land	until	
get	spins	
sled	hits	
pants	lands	
jackets	bump	
mittens	dumps	